LEFT
BY
THEMSELVES

LEFT BY THEMSELVES

Original title: STRANGER IN THE STORM

by Charles Paul May

Interior illustrations by VICTOR AMBRUS

SCHOLASTIC INC.
New York Toronto London Auckland Sydney

*To Catherine Owens Peare
and to James S. Stewart*

ISBN 0-590-45728-4

Text copyright © 1972 by Charles Paul May. Illustrations copyright © 1972 by HarperCollins, Inc. All rights reserved. Published by Scholastic Inc., 730 Broadway, New York, NY 10003, by arrangement with HarperCollins, Inc.

12 11 10 9 8 7 6 5 4 3 2 1   11   2 3 4 5 6 7/9

Contents

Chapter One

A Lot of Snow

Adella Lindsay thought she had never seen so much snow. It lay in ridges along the window ledges and piled up on the west side of tree trunks. The wind whipped it into mounds that grew higher and higher. A sparrow seemed to drop from the pine tree at the corner of the house, then fought its way toward the barn. As it flew just above the ground, Adella lost sight of it among the swirling flakes.

"Do you see your father, Dell?" Mrs. Lindsay asked.

Adella pressed her face to the icy window. "No. No, I can't see him. Do you need him, Mom?" Her voice showed alarm.

"Oh no," her mother answered. She came to Adella's side and let her hand fall lightly on the girl's head. Together they watched the snow as it whirled away in the wind. "There's nothing to worry about, Dell. The baby won't be born for a few days yet." A minute later Mrs. Lindsay turned back to her armchair, settling into it slowly, with a sigh.

Somewhere a dog with a deep voice barked. Adella jumped, and Mrs. Lindsay sat very straight in her chair. Another dog answered. They sounded as if they were on the Lindsay farm. Would anyone be hunting in such a storm? Adella didn't know, for Iowa farm life was new to her.

I don't believe it ever snowed like this in the city, Adella thought. Maybe we should have stayed in Chicago until after the baby was born. Everyone said Dad should stay until spring. Now I see why. But he wouldn't listen. He wanted to move and get used to our new home before the outdoor work started.

Again the dogs barked, sounding as if they were in the orchard. Adella ran to the back bedroom. She could see only the dark outlines of the nearest apple trees. A dog would need long legs to get through the drifts.

Suddenly one of the tree trunks seemed to split in two. Half of it ran to join another trunk. As Adella stared out the window, a huge, dark shape leaped over a snow drift and slipped behind a third tree.

It looks like a bear, Adella thought. I hope it won't attack Dad. Please bear, don't hurt Dad!

Woo—woo—woorf! The dogs again. And the shadowlike figure struggled off through the storm as if the dogs were following on its heels.

Adella felt better. Thank goodness for the dogs. She ran to the kitchen to try to keep the figure in sight, but all she could see was the outhouse. Could the bear be hiding behind there? Or inside? Wherever it was, the dogs would probably drive it away.

"Dell," called Mrs. Lindsay. "What are you doing? Can you see your father? Dell?"

"No, I can't see him," Adella answered as she hurried to her mother's side. She decided not to mention the bear. It might frighten her mother.

"He must be having trouble with the horses," Mrs. Lindsay said. "I don't really need to go to the doctor's house. This storm will end soon. But your father is afraid the snow will get deep and cut us off from town.

He's ready to call this the Great Blizzard of 1850. Just like a city man. If we weren't almost out of food, I'd put my foot down."

Adella smiled. A lot of good it did to put your foot down with her father. He went right ahead and did what he wanted to do.

"I still don't see why I can't ride into Salem with you," Adella said. "Why do I need to stay with Rhoda Pexton until Dad comes back for me? I hate her."

"Why, Dell, what a thing to say. I thought you and Rhoda were becoming friends."

"You can't be friends with her," Adella said. "She's too busy telling me how stupid I am."

Mrs. Lindsay laughed. "When it comes to the farm, we are stupid, I guess. Rhoda can't understand that, for she's never lived anywhere else. Next year I hope to open a school for the farm children around here. Then we'll show her we know a few things she doesn't know."

"She thinks I'm a coward, too," Adella said. "Just because she's not afraid of the cows or horses. She bosses them around just like she does me and her little brothers. She hates her little brothers, you know."

"Oh, now, I doubt that," Mrs. Lindsay objected.

"Then why's she always finding fault with them?" Adella asked.

"When your father finds fault with you or me, does it mean he hates us?" Mrs. Lindsay asked.

"No, of course not," Adella admitted. "But that's different."

"Is it? Why is it different?"

Before Adella could answer, buggy wheels crunched outside in the snow. As Mrs. Lindsay and Adella pulled on their heavy coats and hoods, they heard Mr. Lindsay stamping snow from his boots on the back steps.

"Ready?" he called.

They wrapped wool scarves around their faces until only their eyes showed, and Mr. Lindsay helped them into the buggy. When they were settled under blankets, he slapped the horses lightly with the reins. The horses picked their way slowly down the lane toward the road to town.

"Dad?" Adella said.

Mr. Lindsay only grunted. When one of the horses slipped, he called softly, "Easy, boy, easy." He held the reins tight but urged the horses on with gentle words.

"Why can't I ride into Salem with you?" Adella

asked. There was no answer. Adella looked to her mother.

"Look how slowly we're going," Mrs. Lindsay said. "There is no need for you to be cold for hours. You'll be better off with the Pextons. You and Rhoda can play with her cornhusk dolls."

"But—" Adella started to object. Her father turned his head in her direction. She could see only his eyes above his scarf, but they warned her to say no more. She leaned back on the leather seat. She would stay with Rhoda Pexton. She would be miserable and lonely with that hateful girl, but she would stay until her father came for her.

When they reached the road, he started to turn the horses toward the Pexton farm. The house was half a mile away. Salem lay in the other direction. It would be better if she walked to the Pexton house and let her father go toward town.

"I can walk," Adella told him. "The snow isn't so deep here in the road. And you can get to town quicker." She threw off her blanket and slid to the side of the buggy.

"Oh no," her mother objected.

"Are you sure?" asked Mr. Lindsay.

"Sure," Adella answered. He stopped the horses and Adella jumped to the ground. The snow came halfway to her knees. Mrs. Lindsay protested, but Adella took high steps and started down the road.

"I think it's too deep for you, Dell," her father called after her. "Get back in, and—" He didn't finish. Adella looked back and saw him leaning out of the buggy. He held a hand above his eyes to shield them against the snow. "Someone's coming," he said. "It looks like Rhoda. She'll give you a hand. You'll be all right now, and I'll come for you tonight. Good-bye."

"Good-bye, Dell. Be a good girl," Mrs. Lindsay called.

"I will. Good-bye," Adella answered.

As she heard the buggy go toward town, she felt all alone. She couldn't see Rhoda yet, but her father had said someone was coming. The thought of Rhoda made her feel a little better. Even being with bossy Rhoda would be better than being alone. After all, Rhoda wasn't afraid of anything, probably not even bears.

Remembering the bear in the orchard, Adella took high steps and tried to hurry.

Chapter Two

The Dogs Again

For a minute, walking through the snow seemed like fun. Adella felt like a giant wading across an ocean. Or at least across Lake Michigan, she thought. When I get to the other side, there will be Chicago.

Soon the backs of her legs began to ache. Lifting her feet high with each step tired her, so she started to drag them through the snow instead. It felt as if the snow held onto her boots. The Great Blizzard of 1850 is right, she told herself.

Where is that Rhoda? Adella held her hand over her

eyes as her father had done to shield them from the snow. She saw a figure down the road and tried to hurry. The snow tripped her, and she plunged forward on her face.

As she lay there, Adella heard the dogs barking. They were nearer than they had been before. They sounded as if they might be coming her way.

Adella jumped to her feet and ran. The dark form ahead began to take shape. It was Rhoda. But she was just standing there. Why doesn't she come meet me? Adella wondered.

As she got closer, Adella saw that Rhoda was looking off into the field beside the road. Just like Rhoda, Adella thought. She doesn't even know I'm here. What a hateful girl she is.

"Rhoda!" she yelled. Rhoda jumped like a frightened rabbit.

"Don't shout like that," Rhoda said. "I ain't done nothin'."

"I'll say you haven't," Adella snapped. "Give me a hand. What were you watching?"

"Birds," Rhoda answered. "Did you see them?" Adella shook her head. "They flew just above the ground. You know what that means?"

Adella had no idea, and she didn't much care at this point. She shook her head again.

"Birds flyin' low, there will come snow," Rhoda chanted.

Adella couldn't help but laugh, which made the other girl look angry.

"I don't need birds to tell me that," Adella said. "What's this all over me? All over you? All over the road? Maybe even all over Chicago? I don't need birds to tell me it's snowing."

"Oh, you and your old Chicago," Rhoda said. "I'll bet it ain't bigger than Salem. Anyhow, those birds flyin' low mean there'll be more snow. More and more and more. What do you think of that, Miss City Child?" Before Adella could answer, Rhoda thought of something else. "Anyhow, how come you're out here all by yourself like this?"

"I'm coming to your house," Adella told her. "What are you doing out here?"

"I'm a-comin' to your house," she said. "Since you Lindsays don't know a thimbleful about farmin', Pa sent me to tell you to get your horses and cows in the barn. He's out after ours right now."

"My goodness, the poor cows!" Adella said. "We

were so busy getting Mom ready to stay in town we never thought of the cows. Can you help me find them, Rhoda? Please?"

"Oh, sure," said Rhoda. "Cows can be found easy in weather like this. Either they get behind a building or they drift along with the wind till they come to a fence. Then they stand there, hunched up, tails to the wind. The wind is from the west. If they ain't on the east side of your barn, they'll probably be down in your orchard. Come on." She grabbed Adella's hand and pulled her along.

With her hand in Rhoda's, Adella found it a little easier to walk through the snow. She was glad Rhoda was bigger and older than she was. Rhoda was nearly ten. I won't be ten for almost two years, Adella thought. I wonder if I'll be tall like Rhoda.

"It's shorter if we cut across the field," Rhoda said. They climbed the fence and headed toward the barn. Adella wondered if they had made a mistake. Drifts covered the field. Even Rhoda, with her long legs, had trouble. Being heavier, she sank deeper into the snow than Adella did. In a few minutes they had to stop and rest.

Dogs barked. Adella and Rhoda both jumped. Rhoda pulled her coat tighter about her plump body and started on.

"I don't like the sound of those dogs," Rhoda whispered. "They ain't from around here. Pa said so."

"What do they mean?" Adella asked.

"Don't mean nothin' far as I know," Rhoda answered.

Adella smiled. "Dogs barking low, there will come snow," she giggled.

Rhoda jerked her hand out of Adella's grasp. "All right, Miss City Child. When the snow gets ten million billion feet over your head, you won't think it's so funny." She bounded away across a drift.

Adella ran after Rhoda, slipped, and fell. She wasn't sure she wanted to get up. She felt as if she could go to sleep.

"All right, you silly city child." Rhoda's firm hands caught her by the shoulders. "Get your face up off that ground. You'll never get to heaven lookin' down. That's what Pa always says."

When they reached the barn, the cows weren't there. They struggled to open a door so they could step inside to rest. Rustling sounds came from the hayloft. Adella looked quickly about and drew near to Rhoda.

"Don't be so frighty," Rhoda told her. "Them's only mice or rats."

"Rats?"

"Rats," Rhoda repeated. "Anywhere you keep corn or other grain you'll have mice and rats. Pa takes a board and brains 'em if he can reach 'em. One whack and they don't ever move again. I'll bet I could do it too, if I got near one, but they always run. They're as scared of you as you are of them. That's what Pa always says."

"Let's go look for the cows," Adella said. She thought a little smile flickered across Rhoda's lips, but she wasn't sure. Maybe Rhoda was just teasing her about there being rats in the barn.

In the orchard, drifts stood high. The girls fought their way through. Rhoda went first, but she took long steps that Adella couldn't equal. Adella's back as well as her legs ached. She called for Rhoda to stop.

"Now what's the matter?" Rhoda demanded. "I suppose you're hearin' more rats. Or maybe an elephant?"

That made Adella think of the bear. It had been

24

right here in the orchard! She leaped to Rhoda's side, knocked against her, and caused them both to sprawl in the snow.

"Stupid city child!" Rhoda snapped. "What in the world ails you?" She got to her feet but made no effort to help Adella.

"I saw a bear," Adella said, getting slowly to her feet. Rhoda looked quickly around. She turned back to Adella with a frown. "Right here among the apple trees," Adella added.

"When?" Rhoda asked. She didn't seem to believe it.

"Before I met you on the road," Adella told her.

"You sure don't know a thimbleful about animals," Rhoda said. "This is the first week in December. Bears have been asleep in their dens for a month. Come on."

"But I saw it," Adella insisted. "It was up on its hind legs running from tree to tree."

Rhoda tromped off through the orchard, and Adella had to run to keep up. "I mean it, Rhoda," she panted.

"You're sure it wasn't a giraffe?" Rhoda asked.

"It *was* a bear!" Adella shouted.

"Or maybe a kangaroo," Rhoda snickered. "You've

sure got to look out for the giraffes and kangaroos here in Iowa."

Oh, you old smarty cow, Adella thought to herself. I hate you! I hate you more than I hate rats or bears. But she followed close behind Rhoda, glancing back from time to time to be sure no bear followed them.

At the foot of the orchard, the two cows stood against the fence rails. Their backs were hunched up and their tails were toward the wind. When the girls tried to drive them toward the barn, they didn't want to face into the storm. They would have circled back, but Rhoda leaped and yelled and waved her arms. Adella copied her. She felt better as the jumping and waving warmed her, but she soon grew tired. The cows moved slowly toward the barn, the girls following.

Rhoda stopped short, and Adella bumped into her. Rhoda walked quickly back to the fence and climbed up on it.

"What's—" Adella started to ask, but Rhoda held her finger in front of her scarf where her lips would be. She motioned for Adella to come to the fence. Adella climbed up too.

Looking where Rhoda pointed, Adella saw two

horses. Just beyond them stood a haystack, where two men poked about with sticks. Both men carried long-barrelled guns, and two large dogs were digging their way into the hay.

Chapter Three

Leg Trouble

Adella looked at Rhoda to ask what was happening. The older girl shrugged and shook her head. The men seemed to be shouting, but the wind carried their words away. One man caught the dogs by their collars and pulled them back. The other man raised his gun to his shoulder.

BAM! He fired into the hay. The men and dogs waited, but nothing happened.

"He's crazy," Rhoda whispered. "Let's go before he shoots in this direction."

Adella and Rhoda followed close behind the cows. Every few steps they looked nervously over their shoulders, but the men and dogs had not seen them and were not following.

Halfway across the orchard,the cows and girls came to the biggest drift yet. Slipping and pawing, the cows got over it. Rhoda stayed in their path, but she slipped and fell back. After Adella helped her up, Rhoda tried again. She slipped and fell on her knees. Without trying to get up this time, she crawled through the snow on her hands and knees.

Adella tried to follow, but she too slipped and fell. Even on her hands and knees she kept slipping back. What could she do? Fear seemed to fall upon her, heavier than a drift of snow. She scrambled to her feet. She ran at the white ridge, but her feet flew out from under her. She sat in the snow, in a daze. For all she cared, the dogs could come eat her up. Or a bear. What difference did it make? She was going to sleep.

Something scratched against Adella's arm. The dead branch of a tree seemed to reach out of the storm toward her. She stared at it through half-closed eyes.

"Dell!" Rhoda shouted. Adella shook, as if coming

out of a dream. She stood up and caught hold of the branch. Rhoda, on the other end of it, pulled hard. Slipping and stumbling, Adella got across the drift.

The two girls struggled on. At last they saw a grey shape ahead. The barn. The cows went faster now. Adella and Rhoda couldn't keep up. The trail the cows made began to fill up as soon as the animals passed.

For a minute the sight of the barn gave Adella new hope. But more drifts stood in the way.

"I can't walk anymore," she cried. "Rhoda, I don't think I can take another step. My legs hurt so."

"Good," Rhoda said. "It's when they don't hurt, you want to get worried. Then they're frozen. Move on."

Adella just stood there. "I wish Mom were here."

"If I bring my boot up under your bottom, you'll think a wild horse is here," Rhoda said. She drew back her foot as if to kick. "You'll sail right over that drift."

In spite of her pains Adella felt her lips curl into a little smile. "Dell flying low, there will come snow," she said. Even Rhoda giggled slightly. Feeling a little better, they stumbled on, crawling over drifts on their hands and knees.

At the barn they had to struggle with the door. The

hinges squeaked, as if trying to outcry the wind. At last the door swung open. The first cow was in such a hurry to get into the barn, she knocked Rhoda down.

"Such manners," Rhoda mumbled. "Must be a city cow."

Adella burst into laughter. Rhoda did too. Adella laughed harder, and so did Rhoda. They couldn't stop. They laughed so hard they couldn't pull the door shut.

Something crackled behind them. Their laughter stopped instantly as they whirled around. But only the cows were there. One cow had found a partly eaten ear of corn in the manger. The husks on the ear rattled as the cow dragged the cob into her mouth with her rough tongue.

The girls pulled the door shut and hooked it. Rhoda climbed into the loft and tossed down armfuls of hay. After she filled the manger, she went to the corn bin. She got two ears for each cow.

"A little corn, a lot of hay. Cows will live long lives that way. That's what Pa always says. I'm starved myself. Let's go to the house and get something to eat before I try munching on hay." No answer. Adella sat on the dirt floor. "What are you doing, city child?"

"I can't get up," Adella said. "My legs gave way, and I can't get up."

Rhoda moaned. She stared at Adella and shook her head from side to side as if she couldn't believe it. Then she marched to the corn bin, and returned with a scoop shovel over her shoulder.

"You'll need a sleigh ride, Dell," she announced. She shoved open the small barn door that faced toward the house. After setting the shovel in the snow, she helped Adella crawl to it. Adella sat in the scoop while Rhoda tugged at the handle.

It was a slow trip, but gradually they left the barn behind in the storm. When Rhoda stopped to rest, Adella looked over her shoulder and saw Rhoda rubbing her back.

"Can—can't we make it?" Adella asked.

Rhoda caught up the handle and started on. "Of course we can make it," she said, sounding very cheerful. "It's too far to my house, but we can get to yours. It's just a matter of putting one foot ahead of the other. One foot, two foot, bare foot, shoe foot, slick foot, glue foot, square foot, round foot, air foot, ground foot, big foot, small foot, thick foot, tall foot, left foot, right foot,

dark foot, bright foot, clean foot, dirt foot, sock foot, shirt foot . . . uh . . . uh-h-h . . ."

"Is that what your Pa always says?" Adella asked.

Rhoda almost jerked the shovel out from under her. "And here we are!" she cried.

Hopefully, Adella looked over her shoulder, but they weren't at the house. They were at the outhouse. Adella wanted to laugh, but she also wanted to cry. In a muffled voice she said, "This isn't where I live."

"That's the next stop," Rhoda said. "With the snow getting so deep, we'd better use the toilet while we're here."

She tugged at the door, but it didn't budge. With her hands and feet Rhoda scooped and shoved the snow aside. She yanked at the door. It gave a little, but it snapped shut instantly, as if pulled from the inside.

Rhoda jumped back in surprise. Catching the shovel by the handle, she started dragging Adella toward the house as fast as she could.

"Is . . . is there anyone else around?" she panted.

Adella remembered that the bear had run in that direction. "It must be the bear," she whispered.

Chapter Four

Darkness Comes

Rhoda tried to run. Her feet slipped, causing her to twist the shovel. Adella rolled into the snow. Rhoda caught Adella's coat between the shoulders and helped her crawl the last few feet to the house. They bumped up the steps onto the porch and in the back door. With the door bolted Rhoda calmed down.

"You're crazy," Rhoda said. "Bears are all asleep." She got Adella into a chair by the stove in the front room. Mr. Lindsay had spread ashes over the coals to bank the fire and keep it burning slowly until he came home. Now Rhoda raked the ashes away and added wood. Soon flames leaped brightly in the stove, and the room grew warmer.

"What were those men hunting in that haystack if it wasn't bears?" Adella asked.

"They're crazy too," Rhoda said. "Probably come from Chicago." She closed the doors to the other rooms to keep the heat in the front room. The two girls munched on apples and dry bread.

"You mean this is all there is in the house to eat?" Rhoda asked.

Adella nodded. "That's one reason Dad had to go to town," she said. "We ate the last of the eggs and potatoes for breakfast."

"You silly city folk," Rhoda said, shaking her head.

After they ate, the girls grew sleepy. The warmth of the fire felt so good they nodded and dozed off. Not until the room became chilly again did they waken. Rhoda added more wood to the fire before she went to the window to look out.

"Birds still flyin' low," she muttered.

Adella tried her legs. They hurt, but she could limp to the other girl's side. The snow looked much deeper than when they had come from the barn to the house.

It was all they could do to see the pine tree through the falling flakes.

"Night is coming," Adella said. Rhoda nodded.

"Dad has had time to get to Salem and come back," Adella added. Rhoda nodded again. "He—he will get back, won't he?" the younger girl asked.

"Depends," Rhoda said. Adella waited for her to go on, but the older girl stood silently watching the storm.

"It depends on what?" Adella demanded.

"If he tries to come in the buggy, he won't make it," Rhoda said. "On horseback, he might. Is he a good rider?"

Adella didn't know, so she didn't say anything. They watched the snow some more.

Adella pressed an ear to the window. "What was that?" They listened, but there was no sound. "It sounded like a cow mooing." Still no sound. "Oh, I know. It's time to milk again. The cows' bags will be full."

Rhoda snorted. "You sure don't know a thimbleful about cows," she said. "During storms, they don't give much milk. Still, I'd better find the shovel before it's buried under the snow. I think I'll start a path out to the barn. The more I shovel tonight, the less I'll have to shovel tomorrow, maybe."

"What about the bear?" Adella whispered. Rhoda gave her a look of scorn. "I mean, whatever is out there," Adella said.

"Don't go tryin' to scare me again," Rhoda said. "I

ain't a coward like you. There's nothin' out there. It was just your imagination."

"My imagination? You're the one who couldn't open the outhouse door."

"Just your imagination!" Rhoda snapped. That seemed to close the subject.

"Shouldn't you rest a bit more?" Adella suggested.

"Rest twice tomorrow, you'll have less sorrow. That's what Pa al—Oh well, forget it." She took her coat from where it had been drying across the back of a chair and pulled it on. In the kitchen she put on her boots. With her scarf up to her eyes, she went out of the back door.

A minute later a loud clatter came from the porch. Adella held her breath, too startled to move for a second. As she reached for the door handle, she heard Rhoda's voice, high and frightened.

"Don't shoot," Rhoda was saying, "I ain't done nothin'."

Chapter Five

A Surprise

Adella jerked the door open. Rhoda stood in the middle of the porch, the scoop shovel at her feet, her hands over her head. Two big dogs came halfway up the steps, while two armed men sat on horses behind them.

"A house full of girls." One of them laughed. "What do you know about that?"

Adella didn't see what struck him as funny. "What—what—do you want?" she asked.

The laughing man started to say something, but the other poked him in the ribs with his gun barrel.

"Sorry to frighten you, Ma'am," the second man said. "We've lost a slave, and we've come north to look for him. Have you seen a black man, a big one? He's called Tall Tom."

Adella and Rhoda shook their heads. The two men studied them for a minute.

The second man finally nodded, though he didn't so much as smile. "All right, we believe you," he said. "Which way to the nearest town? We can't stay out in this storm any longer."

Rhoda pointed in the direction of Salem. "Four miles," she said.

But the men made no move to go. "If you see this slave, you have to tell us," the second man said. "The new law says you have to return all runaway slaves. So tell your folks not to try to help him get away. Where are your folks?"

"Having a baby," Adella said.

The first man laughed, but the second one still remained quite serious. "You understand about the law?" Adella and Rhoda nodded.

The two men started off, but the one who had laughed reined his horse to a stop. He looked back at the girls with a grin.

"Besides," he said. "You don't want to help no black man. They eat little girls like you for breakfast."

Rhoda squealed.

"Cut that out, Rab," the second man said. "Let's go."

"You're sure you ain't seen Tall Tom?" the grinning man asked.

"I ain't seen him," Rhoda said. "If I see him, I'll sure let you know, and that's the whole hog truth."

As the men rode out of sight, the girls went back in the house and Rhoda bolted the door. She started pulling off her coat.

"Aren't you going to shovel any?" Adella asked.

"I need to rest a bit more," Rhoda said. "And it'll soon be too dark." She kicked off her boots and went to stand by the stove. Finally she said, "Did that bear you thought you saw look like a black man?"

Adella caught her breath. She hadn't thought of that. She had been thinking about the way those two men had fired into the haystack. That didn't seem right to her if they were hunting a man.

"I suppose it might have been a man," Adella said. "I couldn't see well enough to tell. And it could have been this Tall Tom who was holding the door of the outhouse." Her voice was hardly more than a whisper.

"We should have told those men," Rhoda said. "Their dogs surprised me so when they bounded around the corner of the house, I didn't think of it. I wish they'd come back so we could tell 'em. He probably ain't there now, of course. I guess he'd run soon as he thought we'd found his hidin' place." She rubbed her hands briskly along her arms as if suddenly cold. "I sure hope he keeps runnin'."

For a while Adella stood by the window. At last it was too dark for her to see beyond the windowsill. She crossed to the stove and sat down by Rhoda. Through small openings in the door, the fire sent out a bit of light. They didn't bother to light a candle.

"He won't come," Adella finally said.

"I hope not," Rhoda cried. "I sure hope not."

Adella jumped to her feet. "Just because he's not your father!" she shouted.

"Your father? I was thinkin' about the slave!" Rhoda yelled back.

"Oh." Adella sat back down. "I'm sorry I shouted." They sat in silence a while longer.

Rhoda slipped her arm about Adella's shoulders and drew her close. Adella didn't try to pull away.

"No, your father won't come now," Rhoda said. "He

thinks you're safe at my house. And my folks think I'm safe at yours. My mother probably needs me. My seven little brothers all have colds. I should be there helpin' them blow their runny noses."

Her voice sounded soft. Maybe she doesn't hate them as much as I thought, Adella told herself.

Without warning, Rhoda hopped up.

"And I am safe at your house," she laughed. "Two little mice, a-sittin' in the dark. One ate a sparrow." She handed Adella the last apple. "And the other ate a lark." She took a small chunk of bread for herself. One crust of bread was all that remained in the bowl on the table. "Help me get the bedding," Rhoda said. "We'll sleep here by the stove tonight."

After they made mats of bedding on the floor, Rhoda started to undress. Adella stood on one foot and then on the other.

"What's the matter?" Rhoda asked.

"I need to go to the toilet," Adella said.

"Well, you know where it is."

"I'm not going out there," Adella whispered. To sound braver she added, "The snow's too deep."

Rhoda went to the back bedroom and looked under the bed. She pulled out a sort of pail with rounded edges and a handle on it.

"Just as I thought," she said. "A slop jar. You city folks ain't completely stupid. After you use it, go out on the back porch and throw it as far as you can."

"Jar and all?"

"Oh no, silly. Just what's in it. Don't let go of the handle. And don't throw it against the wind, or you may get it back in your face."

"Is it all right to just throw it outdoors?" Adella asked.

"Why not? That's what cows do."

Adella giggled. "I never saw a cow use a slop jar."

Even Rhoda laughed at that. "You don't know what you'll see before this blizzard is over," she said.

At last the girls settled down to sleep. For the first time Adella noticed all the noises caused by the storm. Windows and doors rattled and squeaked. A tree limb bumped and scraped against the roof. Adella shivered. But Rhoda breathed heavily as if already asleep. There must not be anything to worry about. Adella felt safer, thinking Rhoda wasn't afraid of rats or bears or anything.

Chapter Six

Another Surprise

When Adella woke up, a fire blazed in the stove. Rhoda's clothes were gone and Rhoda seemed to be gone also. Adella ran to the window, where dim light entered. It must be morning, though the falling snow made the day seem dark. A scoop of snow flew into the air. Adella could barely see Rhoda's head above the drifts.

Quickly Adella dressed. In the bowl on the table lay the last piece of bread. She reached for it, stopped, then drew back her hand. In the kitchen, she put on her boots. A small scoop for ashes lay by the cook stove, and she picked it up before she went out. Though the snow was deeper, the wind had died down and the day seemed less cold than yesterday. Rhoda looked like a moving snowman. She gave Adella a big smile.

"Two little mice, a-diggin' in the snow. One said 'Stop!' The other said 'No!' "

Adella picked up only a little snow with her small scoop. But she did the best she could. When Rhoda rested, Adella tried to handle the big scoop, but it was too much for her. Even Rhoda didn't fill it full.

A sparrow flew just above their heads. They both turned to watch it out of sight. Rhoda shook her head sadly.

"Birds flying low, there will come snow," Adella chanted. She held out her hand and caught several flakes. "I do believe you're right, country child."

"I thought you'd believe it after a while," Rhoda panted. But she didn't sound angry, as she sometimes did. They shovelled some more.

"The snow on the bottom is the worst part," Adella said. "I can hardly shovel it."

"Of course," Rhoda agreed. "Snow is heavy. What falls on top packs the bottom down." She heaved some more out of the path.

Adella thought about the snow packing down for a moment. She went back to the porch. Holding onto the porch railing, she stepped off carefully into the snow. Although she sank down to her knees, the snow below the surface held her weight. One slow step at a time, she made her way across the snow. Some of yesterday's pain came back to her legs.

"Look, Rhoda," she called. Rhoda looked up in surprise.

"Careful," the older girl warned. "If you sink down, it may take me hours to dig to where you are." She put aside her shovel and tried to crawl up on the packed layer of snow. It wouldn't hold her weight. "I can't do it," she said. "Can you get to the barn?"

"I suppose so," Adella said.

"Can you milk a cow?" Adella shook her head. "No, of course not," Rhoda grumbled. "Well, take a bucket and try. And give them some hay. Tell them I should be able to dig that far in a couple of days. Then they'll get milked." To herself she thought, by then their bags will be so swollen they won't give much.

Adella went back to the house for a milk pail. Rhoda picked up her shovel and scooped some more. When she looked up, Adella stood above her on the snow, pail in one hand, small scoop in the other.

"Are you stuck?" Rhoda asked.

"No," Adella answered. "I was just looking to see if I could see Dad coming."

"Can you?" Rhoda's voice filled with hope.

"No," Adella admitted.

"Then see to the cows," Rhoda snapped. "Just keep puttin' one foot ahead of the other till you get to the barn."

That cheered Adella. She lifted a foot and started off. "Left foot, right foot, day foot, night foot, grey foot, white foot, black foot, blue foot, old foot, new foot, bare foot, shoe foot, square foot, true foot." And finally she reached the barn. She got the door open a crack and squeezed through.

"Good morning, cows," Adella greeted them. "Are you as hungry as I am?" She set the milk pail on the milking stool and looked at the first cow's teats. "I sure wish I knew how to milk you. I'm starved." She felt one of the teats, but the cow lifted her foot. Adella jumped back. "Maybe I'd better just feed you."

The cows had eaten their corn and most of their hay. Adella climbed the ladder into the loft, where only a little light came in through cracks between the boards. Picking up an armful of hay, she tossed it down to the cows. She got another armful and threw it down. When she turned back for more, she saw something dark partly covered with hay at the edge of the pile.

She stepped back quickly. A rat, she thought. I'm getting out of here. As she reached the ladder, she kicked the little scoop that she had laid near it. With the scoop in her hand, she felt a bit braver.

What had Rhoda said? You could brain a rat with a board. If she could do it with a scoop, Rhoda might not think her a coward anymore. She stood shivering, half hoping the rat would run. It's supposed to be as scared as I am, she reminded herself. But it didn't move.

Quietly, slowly, she tiptoed back to the pile of hay. She raised the scoop above her head and brought it down on the grey shape.

"YEE-OWW!" The hay pile seemed to explode in front of her. She fell backward with a shriek. As flying hay and dust settled about her, a figure took shape. It seemed a mile high as she lay propped on her elbows staring up at it. It was a man. A tall, dark man.

With hay in his hair and on his clothes, he looked funny. But not to Adella. All she could think of was the runaway slave, Tall Tom.

Chapter Seven

The Piece of Bread

For a minute longer, Adella lay where she had fallen. When she moved, it was so sudden the man leaped back. She rolled onto her stomach, sprang to her feet, and jumped from the loft onto the hay she had thrown down for the cows. As she reached the barn door, a voice called, "Don't say you've seen me, please."

Outside in the snow she slipped and fell. Scrambling up, she tried to run but fell again. The harder she tried to run, the farther down into the snow she sank. On her feet again, she forced her way through the snow. Twice more she fell. Where was Rhoda? She tried to call, but her breath came in gasps and her voice was a mere squeak.

At last she reached the trench where Rhoda was still scooping snow. Adella slid into the cleared path, sending a shower of snow over the older girl. Before Rhoda could complain, Adella whispered, "He's there. He's in the barn."

"Is he all right?" Rhoda asked as if nothing were the matter. She sounded so calm, Adella felt a little better.

"I guess so," Adella said.

"Then give him the pail and tell him to milk," Rhoda ordered. "Tell him we're hungry." She got no answer to that. "Well, come on, Dell!" she snapped. "Don't just sit there in the snow. We need the milk. And it ain't good to let the cows go too long, even if they don't give much. The milk cakes inside their bags and causes all sorts of trouble."

"If you're so brave, you go tell him," Adella said.

"I would if the snow would hold me," Rhoda told her. "I ain't scared of your father."

"Oh, it's not my father," Adella explained. "It's him! The slave. Tall Tom."

Rhoda's shovel clattered on the frozen ground, and she ran for the house. When Adella got there, snowy tracks led to the back bedroom and under the bed. As

Adella crossed the room, Rhoda's frightened voice whispered, "Don't eat me. I ain't done nothin'."

"It's me," Adella told her, hardly more than whispering herself.

For some time Adella sat on the bed and Rhoda lay under it. But the room was too cold for them to stay still. At last, when nothing happened, Rhoda crawled out and they went to the front room. Rhoda built a big fire, as if it would help keep trouble away.

"There isn't much wood left," Adella warned. Rhoda shrugged and added another piece to the fire.

From time to time one girl or the other looked at the bowl holding the bread. Finally, Rhoda picked up the bowl and held it out to Adella. Adella shook her head. Rhoda put the bowl back on the table. They sat in silence while the fire burned down.

"I wonder if he's hungry too," Adella said.

"Who?" Rhoda asked.

"That black man. Tall Tom."

Rhoda drew closer to the stove. "He's probably eaten one of the cows by now," she said. "If he'd eat one of us, he sure wouldn't stop at eatin' a cow."

Adella also stood closer to the fire. In a minute she asked, "Do you really think he'd do that?"

"How would I know?" Rhoda snapped. "I ain't

never seen a black man. Pa says they sometimes go
through Salem on their way north, but he's never said
he's seen one. Have you?"

"Yes, in Chicago." Adella thought about the black
people she'd seen. "They never tried to hurt me that I
know of. And I never heard anyone say a thing against
them like that man said yesterday. He could have been
lying, couldn't he?" She got no answer. "Well, couldn't
he?"

"Let's don't talk about it anymore!" Rhoda ordered.
"I thought he'd sure enough be gone by this mornin'
if it was him. Why didn't he go?"

"The storm didn't seem to worry you yesterday,"
Adella said. "How come you're so scared now?"

"I've seen storms before," Rhoda answered. "We
have 'em here in Iowa all the time. Pa's told me what
to expect of them. I don't know nothin' about slaves or
what they'll do."

Adella thought about that for a while. She couldn't
remember ever having seen a blizzard before. Maybe
that's why the storm worried her more than it did
Rhoda. But the black men and women she'd seen in
Chicago had always been friendly to her. She felt a
little better. At least it wasn't a bear.

Adella went to the window to look out. The day was lighter and she could clearly see the pine tree. The barn was a large grey outline through the falling flakes. Adella thought of the cows. She stamped her foot, making Rhoda jump.

"He has no right to touch one of our cows," Adella said. "I should go tell him he has no right."

"Sure you go tell him that, city child," Rhoda said. "Then he can eat you instead of the cow."

"Oh, I don't believe people eat people," Adella said. "Those men just said that to scare us. Maybe he'll listen if I say please."

"He may not know what the word means," Rhoda said.

"He does too," Adella told her. "He used the word himself. He said, 'Don't say you've seen me, please.' He sounded scared. Just like me." She thought about that for a minute. "He jumped back when I moved, as if he thought *I* was going to hurt *him*." She started pulling her coat on. Rhoda watched her, wide-eyed.

When she was ready, Adella took the last of the bread. Rhoda made no move to stop her. Adella went out of the back door and across the snow. Once she looked around and saw Rhoda at the window. Rhoda

had her coat on; she was ready to come to Adella's aid.

Feeling braver, Adella went on. She opened the barn door slowly, hoping the hinges wouldn't squeak. But they did. The two cows quietly chewing hay looked around at her. The sight of them, so calm and unhurt, gave Adella more courage. She stepped inside the barn. She started for the ladder, then stopped, for the black man stood beside it.

They looked at each other for what seemed to Adella like a long time. Slowly she lifted her arm and held out the bread. "Please don't eat a cow," she said.

"Thank you," Tall Tom said. He put all the bread in his mouth at once. While he chewed, he went to where the milk pail hung on a hook. Taking it down carefully, he brought it to her.

"Can you carry it?" he asked. It was half full of milk. She wanted to laugh. Or to cry. She wasn't sure which. "It'll keep you from starving," he said.

Chapter Eight

A Cold House

"I think I can carry it," Adella said. When she went out into the snow, Tall Tom closed the door behind her.

Rhoda, armed with the shovel, waited for her on the back porch. The older girl looked at the milk as if she didn't believe it was real. They each drank three dippersful and felt better. Rhoda started shovelling snow again.

"But I'm not goin' all the way to the barn," she warned. "You'll have to do the last of it your own self."

"Maybe you'd better dig to the woodpile," Adella suggested. "The milking is done now. But there's not enough wood left to get us through another night."

That made sense, so Rhoda started a new path. After a few scoops, she stopped. She stood on tiptoe and looked across the snow toward the barn. After scooping a bit more, she stopped again.

"He could be up there in the loft watching us from a crack or knothole," Rhoda whispered. "If he's as tall as you say, he could wade right through this snow." She seemed to be shivering. "I'm tired. I need a rest." She left the shovel in the snow and hurried into the house.

The front room was cold, but Rhoda made no move to put more wood in the stove. Adella counted what was left. Five pieces. She took a blanket from where they had slept on the floor and wrapped it around their legs. If only her mom or her dad were there.

"What'll you do if those two men come back for him?" Rhoda asked. Adella hadn't given that any thought. Now she wondered about it. "We'll have to tell them where he is," Rhoda decided.

"Why?" Adella wanted to know.

"Because it's the law," Rhoda answered. "They said so."

"They also said he ate little girls like us," Adella pointed out. "They could be lying about everything."

Rhoda shook her head. "Wasn't the same man what said it. The one man may have been lyin'. Probably was. But the other man, he was serious. He said it was the law. We'll have to tell."

Adella kicked the blanket loose and pulled a little away from Rhoda. "It doesn't seem right to tell," Adella said. "Not after he's done the milking for us."

"It's the law," Rhoda said. "I don't want no trouble with the law. If they ask me where he is, I'll tell."

"Well-l-l-l, I—I'm not sure I will," said Adella. "Oh, I wish Mom were here." She sounded lost.

Rhoda put her arm across Adella's shoulders. "You can call me Momma Mouse," she giggled.

Adella knocked her arm aside and sprang to her feet. "I—I just may call you a—*a knock-kneed, cross-eyed, tattle-tale cow!*" she shouted.

Rhoda's mouth set in a hard, straight line. Her fists clenched as she bobbed to her feet. But tears in Adella's eyes caught her attention. Slowly her hands and her mouth relaxed.

"So that's what I am," she said, a trace of anger in her voice. "I've always wondered what I was." She managed a little smile and started to sing. "I'm a knock-kneed"—she bumped her knees together—

"cross-eyed"— she looked cross-eyed down her nose— "rattle-tail"—she wiggled her bottom— "cow. *MOO!*"

Adella couldn't help but snicker. She took a step toward Rhoda, and another. She threw her arms around Rhoda's waist. "That's the kind of cow I like best," she said. Rhoda's strong arms felt almost as good as her mother's.

Rhoda couldn't tell if Adella was laughing or crying. They sat down and pulled the blanket over their legs. In five minutes both girls were asleep.

Cold and hunger awakened Adella. The fire was almost out. Without waiting for Rhoda to do it, she put a piece of wood in the stove. Should she put in another? There were so few left. But the room wouldn't get warm on one piece, so she added a second one.

Rhoda's voice surprised her. "We've got to get to the woodpile," Rhoda said. "You can walk across the snow. Do you think you can dig down to the wood when you get there?"

Adella hadn't thought of that before. "I guess I'll have to," she said. She felt better already. Just imagine, Rhoda needed her help instead of her needing Rhoda's.

"Of course I can." And she tossed another piece onto the fire.

It didn't take her long to get ready to go out. She drank a dipper of milk, wiped her lips, and stepped out on the back porch. She almost fell over a stack of wood.

Looking toward the barn, she saw Tall Tom scooping out the path Rhoda had started. She wanted to shout for joy, but she didn't. Instead, she picked up some wood and went back in the house, trying not to smile.

"Here you are," she called.

Rhoda came into the kitchen and took the wood from her. "Good for you," she said. "That was quick. I didn't think you'd be . . . How—did you get this wood so fast?"

Adella laughed too hard to answer, but Rhoda's face remained serious. "Did he—did that . . . Black Tom get it for you?" Rhoda asked.

"Tall Tom," Adella corrected her. "He left it on the porch."

"Oh my," Rhoda said. "Oh my goodness. He's been right up here to the house. And while we were sleepin'. Oh my goodness. What will happen next?"

Chapter Nine

Corn and Ashes

"He's almost to the barn now," Adella announced. She stood at the window, while Rhoda sat by the stove. "Come watch. He really makes that old snow fly."

"I'm watchin' the stove," Rhoda said. "You keep an eye on him."

"But you haven't even seen him," Adella objected. "If you saw him, you'd see he's just a big man like any other big man. You wouldn't be scared anymore."

"I'm not scared," Rhoda denied. "I just got cold when the fire died down. I'm just tryin' to get warm again. Nothin' wrong with that, is there?"

"You've sat by that fire until you're half cooked," Adella said. "If it weren't for him, you'd be a lot colder and a lot hungrier. We may owe our lives to him. You could at least go out and say thanks to him."

"I'll say thanks to him twice tomorrow," Rhoda said. "Or the day after. Maybe they'll come and take him away by then. Is there any milk left?"

"A little. Finish it up. I'm sure he'll milk for us again tonight."

She watched out of the window while Rhoda had a drink of milk. Rhoda didn't go near the window but returned to her chair by the fire.

"How long can we live on milk?" Adella asked.

"I don't know," Rhoda answered. "A long time, I hope. Anyhow, in a day or two Pa will suspect somethin's wrong and come to see. He'll want me there to help with those seven little brothers. I could be rubbin' mustard on their chests. I never get time to be sick. They always beat me to it."

Adella smiled. From the sound of her voice, Rhoda missed being with her little brothers. Maybe she even liked helping look after them.

Adella watched Tall Tom finish the shovelling. After

he disappeared into the barn, she joined Rhoda by the stove. Her stomach growled. Milk was hardly enough to keep her from being hungry.

Her thoughts turned to her mother and father. She silently prayed they had reached Salem safely. Her dad had been right in saying they should go. There would be no way to get the doctor now. She tried to think what it would be like to have a baby brother or sister. But all she could picture were Rhoda's seven brothers.

A noise on the back porch brought both girls to their feet. At the sound of knocking, Rhoda raced into the bedroom. Adella just stood by the stove. The knock came again. She tried to lift her foot, but nothing happened. She could hear the back door opening slowly. She hadn't bolted it after she brought the wood in.

"Girls?" She knew it was Tall Tom's voice. "Girls," he called again. "I've brought you something to eat."

Food! As if drawn by a magic word, Adella started toward the door to the kitchen. She opened it and peeked in. Looking in the back door was Tall Tom. He smiled when he saw her, and he held out a small basket.

"Oh, thank you, Tall Tom," Adella said. She, too,

smiled until she took the basket from his hand. It was full of corn. Hard kernels of corn. She would break her teeth trying to eat those.

But Tall Tom still smiled. In his other hand he carried a wooden box. "Do you have a large crock?" he asked.

Out of the cupboard, she got a metal pan. He said it wouldn't do, and she soon found a pottery crock. He placed the crock in the sink and set the wooden box on top of it. From his hip pocket, he took the little scoop Adella had dropped in the hay loft. He scooped ashes from the cook stove and dumped them in the box. Adella watched everything he did.

Tall Tom dipped water from the tank on the cook stove. He poured this slowly over the ashes. When he lifted the box a little, Adella could see the water dripping through cracks in the bottom of the box. He put more ashes in the box and poured more water over them. In time he had a crock nearly full of water.

"Lye water," he said. "The water takes something out of wood ashes and becomes lye water." He dropped a handful of corn into the water. He asked for a wooden spoon, which Adella found, and he stirred

the corn with this. The outer skins of the kernels came off and floated to the top. Tall Tom scooped them out of the water. Without their skins, the kernels swelled up to make soft, white lumps.

"That's hominy," Tall Tom said. "It's good to eat."

Chapter Ten

Hominy Breakfast

"Hominy," Adella repeated. "I can hardly wait to try it."

Tall Tom laughed. "But you have to wait. Lye water is poison, so you have to wash it off the hominy before you eat any. You need to rinse it and rinse it and rinse it again in clear water. Then you let it soak overnight in more clear water. In fact, you'd better get the cleanest snow you can find and melt it in the tank on the stove. It takes lots of clean, clear water to make hominy."

While Tall Tom worked at the sink, Adella noticed he wore an ordinary pair of work shoes. Her father kept an old pair of boots in a closet off the kitchen, but Tall Tom's feet wouldn't fit into them. She did find two pair of heavy socks he could stretch over his feet. She also found a pair of gloves he could wear, but he was too big for other clothes except a wool scarf.

As he fixed a big bowl of hominy, Tom became more talkative. "What town is this near?" he wanted to know.

"Salem."

"Salem what?" he asked.

"Iowa," she told him. Didn't everybody know where Salem was? Everybody knew where Chicago was.

"That's good," he said "I'm across the border. All I've got to do is keep going north. The farther I get from Missouri, the safer I'll be. I don't think they'll keep after me in this blizzard. Is Canada far?"

Adella had no idea. "It must be," she said. "I think it must be many miles."

"I'm sure it is," he agreed. "When I get across that border, I'm really safe."

"What do you mean?" Adella asked.

Tall Tom lowered his voice as if afraid someone else might be listening. "I've run away from the man who owns me. And there's a law that says you have to return a slave to his owner if you catch him. It holds good here in Iowa. Canada's another country. The law doesn't work there, and he can't come after me."

"Why did you run away?" she asked.

"To be free," he said. "Some slaves run away from beatings. Some want to escape work that's too hard for them. But the main thing we all want is to be free. I wasn't beaten. I'm strong enough to do any work they gave me. But I wasn't free. I want to come and go like other men."

Adella nodded. "Like the black people I saw in Chicago?" she asked. "They came and went without owners."

"That's what I want," he said. "Some men buy their freedom. Some have it given to them. But I don't plan to wait any longer. Besides, it may never come. I want to get away right now." As if fearing he had talked too much, he turned quickly to the door. "I'll do the milking for you. What became of your friend?"

"Oh, she—I think she went to bed."

As soon as he was gone, Adella ran to find Rhoda.

77

The older girl crawled slowly from under the bed. She got to her feet as if stiff and sore.

"I hope you had a lovely chat," Rhoda snarled. "Why didn't you serve tea? Why didn't you quilt a quilt? Why didn't you raise a barn?"

"I never once thought of it," Adella snapped back. "But he'll be in with the milk. Then we can do all those things. I'm glad you suggested them."

She went to the kitchen to melt snow and rinse the hominy. When Rhoda saw the heaping bowl of food, her tone grew softer. She knew what hominy was and helped with the work until they heard footsteps on the porch. In a rush Rhoda left the room.

Tall Tom handed in the milk and started back to the barn. Adella said he could sleep in the kitchen by the stove, but he laughed and shook his head.

"I know more about barns," he said.

"But you'll sleep better here," Adella told him.

"More reason not to," he said. "It's not safe to sleep well when you're running. Besides, I slept last night."

The next morning, Adella awoke to the smell of cooking. It was a strange, half sweet, half sour smell, and she guessed it was the hominy. As soon as she

dressed, she went to the kitchen and found Rhoda at the stove.

"There's a little butter, and we've got lots of salt," Rhoda said. "Bring me your plate."

In a minute they were eating. The hominy tasted delicious. At first, Adella thought she could eat all of it by herself. But before long her stomach seemed very full. When they finished, Rhoda started filling another plate.

"Go call that man," she said. But as Adella went to the door, she stopped her. "No, you'd better fetch him in. If you call, no tellin' who's around to hear you. I'll stay in the front room while he eats."

The path to the barn was partly full of snow. The flakes must have been falling all night, Adella thought. When she reached the barn, Tall Tom didn't answer. She looked in the corn bin and the hay loft, but he was gone. Adella ran back to the house to tell Rhoda. If Rhoda was sorry, she didn't show it. They heated water on the stove and washed the dishes.

"I'll throw this lye water out and make some more," Rhoda said. "You're sure you watched just how he did it? We don't want to do nothin' wrong."

"I'm sure," Adella said.

Rhoda stepped out the back door. A moment later a loud crash came from the porch. Adella held her breath for a second. As she reached for the door handle, she heard Rhoda's voice, high and frightened.

"Don't shoot," Rhoda was saying. "I ain't done nothin'."

Chapter Eleven

A Broken Crock

Adella jerked the door open. Rhoda stood in the middle of the porch, pieces of broken crock at her feet, her hands above her head. The two big dogs came halfway up the steps, while the two armed men sat on their horses behind them.

"Oh, sure, I know where we are now," the first man said. "It's that house full of little girls."

"And—and you can see, we . . . we haven't been

eaten," said Adella. She wanted to sound brave, but she couldn't keep her voice steady.

"You're mighty lucky," the man said, showing his teeth in a big grin. He looked right at Rhoda. "And you ain't seen a runaway slave?"

Adella wanted to answer for her, but Rhoda didn't give her a chance.

"I ain't set eyes on nobody but this here brave city child," Rhoda said. "And that's the whole hog truth."

The men sat on their horses, studying the two girls. Adella and Rhoda grew braver and glared back at them. Finally, the second man pulled his horse's reins.

"Come on, Rab. We might as well head home. We just wasted time waiting around in Salem for this blizzard to end. The dogs can't pick up a trail in all this snow."

But the first man still sat there. "I think we ought to look around first," he said. "What's in the barn, girls?"

"Cows," Adella said. "And don't you bother them. They're giving very little milk as it is because of the storm."

"That so?" said the man, still grinning.

"That's so," Adella said. "You sure don't know a

thimbleful about farming if you don't know that."
She thought Rhoda giggled, but she wasn't sure.

"But you don't mind if we look around?" the man
asked.

Would they find tracks in the snow? Rhoda answered
before Adella could think of what to say. "Course
not," Rhoda said as she bent to pick up a piece of the
broken pottery. "You can look all you want, just as
soon as you pay for this here crock."

Both men looked surprised. Then the first one
laughed. "You broke the crock, clumsy. We had
nothin'—"

The piece of pottery flew through the air, straight
at his head. He threw up his arm to shield his face,
jerking the reins. His startled horse reared, wheeled
about, and raced off toward the orchard. Rhoda picked
up another piece of crock, but the second man spoke
to his horse and followed the first one. The dogs
bounded after him, having trouble in the deep snow.
Soon they all disappeared from sight among the trees.

"With luck, we're rid of them," Rhoda said. She
kicked at a piece of crock. "Look how I messed that
up. Now how do we make more hominy?"

"It doesn't matter," Adella said. She threw her arms around Rhoda. "You said the right things. Oh, thank you, thank you, Rhoda."

"Don't thank me," Rhoda said. "I ain't done nothin'."

Chapter Twelve

Birds Flying High

With Tall Tom gone, Rhoda did the milking. And the two girls together worked to clear the path before the snow got too deep again.

Once, while she was resting, Rhoda pointed up. "Look, look!" she cried. Adella looked but saw nothing. Only a sparrow was flying overhead from the barn to the pine tree. "Did you see it?" Rhoda asked, her voice full of excitement.

"I didn't see anything but a bird," Adella answered, still looking up.

"But that's it!" Rhoda said. "That's it. It was way above our heads. Birds flyin' high, comes a clear sky."

"Oh," Adella sighed. She began to feel hopeful.

"At least that's what Pa always says," Rhoda told her.

"Then I'm sure it's true," Adella said. They bent over their shovels and worked hard.

By the time they neared the barn, Adella's back ached. She could barely lift the small scoop high enough to empty it. Finally, it caught on something. She looked up, right into her father's eyes.

"Dad! Dad!" She was up in his arms, clawing off his scarf, covering his face with kisses.

In the house Mr. Lindsay had a sack of food that he had carried from town on foot. He fixed the girls a lunch of bacon and eggs. While he worked, he told them that the trip to town in the buggy had made the baby arrive early. It was a healthy boy, but Adella's mother couldn't come home with it until the snow melted enough for them to come in the buggy.

"A boy!" Adella shouted. "Did you hear that, Rhoda? I have a baby brother."

"Good for you," Rhoda said. "Wait till you have seven. You can help them blow their runny noses."

Mr. Lindsay laughed. Adella realized Rhoda was pleased in spite of her funny words.

While they ate, the girls told Mr. Lindsay of the storm, the cows, and Tall Tom.

He chuckled. "Some day," he said, "you can tell your children what happened to you in the Great Blizzard of 1850."

"Is there a law that says we have to return slaves?" Rhoda asked. "Or was that as big a lie as the one about Tall Tom eating us for breakfast?"

"The part about the law is true," Mr. Lindsay told them. "It's called the Fugitive Slave Law. 'Fugitive' means 'runaway.' It was passed earlier this year, but many people feel it is unfair. There are people in Salem who help the runaways go north. They say slavery should be against the law. So they don't feel they break the law when they help a slave. I don't know whether they're right or not."

"What would you have done?" Adella asked.

"I guess I'd have done what you did," Mr. Lindsay said.

After they ate, Mr. Lindsay took Adella on his shoulders. He held Rhoda by the hand, and slowly they made their way toward Rhoda's house. The closer they got to the Pexton house, the faster Rhoda tried to go. She would have fallen had not Mr. Lindsay held her up. When they got there, Rhoda rushed inside.

"Horace, Elmer, Waldo, Mortimer, Daniel, Matthew, Scratchy, I'm home," she shouted. There were answering shouts of joy.

"We'd better not go in if they have colds," Mr. Lindsay said. They talked to Mr. and Mrs. Pexton on the porch for a few minutes.

When Mr. Lindsay started for home, Adella looked back. She saw Rhoda at a window of the house. The older girl had a little boy in her arms. Both Rhoda and the boy waved. Adella waved back.

"I hope I can see you soon," Adella called.

"Every day you want," Rhoda answered. "We can play we're two little mice lost in the snow."

As they neared home, Mr. Lindsay said, "I thought your mother said you didn't like Rhoda."

"Me, not like Rhoda?" Adella asked in surprise. Then she remembered what she had told her mother about hating the older girl. That seemed so long ago. "Well-l-l . . . she's a little different than I thought. She can be brave and cheerful. And good to her little brothers, too. How could anybody not like Rhoda?" When he chuckled, she did too.

For a time Adella rode quietly on her father's shoulders. "Dad?" she said after a while.

"Yes, Dell."

"Will he really get away?"

"Who?" her father asked.

"Tall Tom. Will he make it to Canada?"

"We have no way of knowing," he told her. "We can only hope he does. If he can reach the right people around Salem, they'll help him make it. And since those two men with the dogs turned back, there's a good chance he'll win his freedom."

He was quiet for several steps. Finally, he said, "During your life, a lot of people will come and go. You'll see them for a few weeks, or a few years. Then they'll move on or you'll go away. Some you'll hear from again, some you never will. That's life. You can't hold on to everybody."

Adella looked back toward the Pexton house. "I don't want to hold on to everybody," she decided. "But I hope I can hold on to Rhoda for a long, long time."

She noticed something for the first time. "Dad, look! It's stopped snowing."

"Well, so it has," he agreed. "I thought it never would."

"Oh, it had to," Adella told him. "The birds and Rhoda said it did. These last three days, I've learned a thimbleful about weather."